URASHIMA TARO
and Other
Japanese Children's Stories

URASHIMA TARO
and Other
Japanese Children's Stories

edited by
Florence Sakade

illustrated by
Yoshio Hayashi

CHARLES E. TUTTLE COMPANY

Rutland, Vermont   *Tokyo, Japan*

Published by the Charles E. Tuttle Company, Inc.,
of Rutland, Vermont & Tokyo, Japan
with editorial offices at Suido 1-chome, 2–6, Bunkyo-ku, Tokyo

International Standard Book No. 0–8048–0609–8

First edition, 1964
Seventeenth printing, 1988

PRINTED IN JAPAN

Stories in This Book

Publisher's Foreword

In 1952 we published the first edition of *Japanese Children's Stories from Silver Bells*, one of Japan's leading children's magazines. Since then, although the magazine is no longer published, the book has been so popular that successive reprintings have worn the plates past further use, and still orders pour in for it. To meet this continuing demand, we have now issued a revised edition of the book with entirely new illustrations and several new stories, in a single volume entitled *Japanese Children's Stories*, and also in two companion volumes entitled *Urashima Taro* and *Kintaro's Adventures*. We are confident these books will meet the same enthusiastic response as did the first edition.

A child who has been given a feeling of sympathy for the children of another country is on the way to becoming a true world citizen. For that reason those stories have been chosen with Japanese backgrounds which will both give the Western child a sense of identity with Japanese children and also explain some of the different customs. Indeed, it is this Japanese flavor which makes the stories appeal to older children at the same time as the stories remain simple enough for young children. And the illustrations are noteworthy for their Japanese flavor, serving as an introduction to the remarkable talent the Japanese artist has always possessed in the realms of line, color, and form.

Most of the stories are retellings of traditional Japanese stories, beloved through many generations, similar to those introduced to the English-speaking world by Lafcadio Hearn. But only in the case of "Urashima Taro" has a new version of one of Hearn's renderings been included, and that only because the story is too delightful to be omitted. To make the selection as representative as possible two modern stories have been included, "The Dragon's Tears" and "Why the Red Elf Cried," as well as a completely modern version of a famed classic, "Kintaro's Adventures," all by some of Japan's foremost contemporary storytellers.

Editorial responsibility for the book has been borne by Florence Sakade; both as a mother and as an editor and author of numerous children's publications, she has had wide experience in the entertainment and education of children. The English versions are the work of Meredith Weatherby, well-known translator of Japanese literature.

Urashima Taro

A LONG, long time ago in Japan there was a young fisherman who lived by the seashore. His name was Urashima Taro. One day while he was walking along the beach, he saw that some boys had caught a big turtle from the sea and were teasing it and hitting it with sticks.

Now, Taro was very kind hearted and hated to see people being cruel to animals. So he said: "Boys, please let the turtle go. It's a nice animal and you shouldn't be mean to it. Put it back in the sea."

Then the boys were ashamed of themselves. They put the turtle back in the water and watched it swim happily away.

Several days later, Taro was again walking along the beach when he heard a voice saying: "Taro! Taro!"

He looked around, but couldn't see anyone. "Who is calling me?" he called out.

"Here I am," said a voice from the sea. It was a turtle, who came crawling up on the sand. "I'm the turtle you saved the other day. When I returned to the palace under the sea, I told the Sea Princess what you had done. This made her very happy, and she asked me to bring you to see her."

Taro said: "I've always wanted to visit the bottom of the sea." So he climbed on the turtle's back and was carried off very far and very fast to the great palace on the floor of the deepest sea.

He was taken inside the beautiful palace, which was made of coral and crystal, and there he met the beautiful Sea Princess. "Taro, you were very kind to my good subject, the turtle," she said to him. "I wanted to thank you, so I had him bring you here. Please be my friend and stay in the palace forever. We will be very happy, and you shall have everything you want."

So Taro stayed in the palace with the Sea Princess. He ate wonderful food, saw wonderful things and was very happy at first. But after a while —after only a few days, he thought—he began to be lonely for his home and his friends back on the shore. He wondered how his father and mother were.

Finally, one day he said to the princess: "I've been very happy here, but I want to go back to the land and see my home and my friends. Please send me back."

"All right, Taro," the princess said, "if you are determined to go, then I'll send you back. But I'll be sorry to see you go. We've been so happy together. In memory of your stay here I'll give you this beautiful box. As long as you have this, you may come back to see me anytime you wish. But, Taro, don't open this, ever. If you open it, you'll never be able to come back. Be sure! Do not open it!"

So Taro took the box, thanked the princess for the wonderful time, climbed on the back of the turtle, and went back to his home.

When he got to the beach, the village had changed. He could no longer find his own house. He asked some people on the beach, "Where is Urashima Taro's house, and where are his parents?"

"Why, young man," they answered, "you're asking about things that were here many, many years ago. Urashima Taro was drowned before most of us remember. What strange person are you that you do not know this?"

Taro was very puzzled. How could this be? He was the same—or so he thought—and only the people and the place were different. Could it be that the secret of this strange thing was in the box that the Sea Princess had given him? He thought about this for some time, and then at last he decided to open the box, even though the Sea Princess had warned him not to do so.

He took off the lid, and a strange white smoke came out and curled about him. He touched his face and discovered that his face was all wrinkled and that he had a long white beard. Without realizing it, he had spent many, many years at the bottom of the sea, not just a few days. The magic box had kept him always young, but now the smoke from the box had turned him into the old, old man that he really was. All his friends were gone, and now that he had opened the box he could never return to the palace of the Sea Princess. He stood weeping on the shore.

The Fairy Crane

ONCE upon a time there was an old man who lived in the country all alone with his old wife. They had no children. One .day the old man was walking along the road beside a rice field when he suddenly heard a strange sound: "Flutter, flutter, flap, flap." Following the sound, he discovered a beautiful white crane caught in a snare.

"Oh, you poor thing!" he said. "I will help you out." He set the crane free, and it flew away into the sky.

15

After the old man got home and was telling his wife about the crane, a knock came at the door and someone said in a sweet voice: "May I come in?" The old woman opened the door and there she found a pretty, dainty little girl.

The little girl said: "I have lost my way. Please let me stay in your house tonight."

The old people were very happy to have such a pretty girl in their house. And when she told them that she had no parents of her own, they asked her to become their daughter and live with them always. So the little girl stayed on with them.

One day the girl said to her new parents: "If you'll promise not to look at me even once while I work, I'll weave some cloth on the loom in the weaving room." Thereafter they could hear the sound of the loom every day—"Ton-ka-ra-ri, ton-ka-ra-ri"—and every night the little girl gave them a beautiful piece of cloth which she had woven that day. It was the most beautiful cloth in the whole world and all the neighbors came to see it.

The old woman became more and more curious. She said to herself: "How in the world can this little girl weave such beautiful cloth?" So finally one day she peeked into the weaving room.

What a strange sight she saw! There, sitting at the loom, was not her little daughter but a beautiful white crane, using its own soft white feathers to weave cloth!

That night when the old man came home, the little girl came out of the weaving room and said: "I am the crane that you saved. I have been weaving cloth to repay the kindness you did for me that day long ago. But now that you have discovered my secret, I can no longer stay with you."

The old woman was sorry she had peeked, and the old man was in tears, but since they knew their daughter was actually a crane, they finally understood that she must go back to her home in the sky.

"Goodbye, good luck," the girl said. And then suddenly she changed into a white fairy crane and soared gracefully up into the sky on her beautiful white wings.

The Fairy Crane

The Dragon's Tears

FAR AWAY in a strange country there lived a dragon. And the dragon's home was in a deep mountain cave, from which his eyes shone like headlights. Very often, when some of the people living nearby were gathered in the evening by the fire, one would say: "What a dreadful dragon is living near us!" And another would agree, saying: "Someone should kill him!"

Whenever children were told about the dragon, they were frightened. But there was one little boy who was never frightened. All the neighbors said: "Isn't he a funny little boy!" When it was almost time for this funny little boy's birthday, his mother asked him: "Whom would you like to invite for your birthday party?" Then that little boy said: "Mother, I would like to ask the dragon!" His mother was very much surprised and asked: "Are you joking?" "No," said the little boy very seriously, "I mean what I say: I want to invite the dragon."

And, sure enough, on the day before his birthday the little boy stole quietly out of his house. He walked and he walked and he walked till he reached the mountain where the dragon lived.

"Hello! Hello! Mr. Dragon!" the little boy called down the valley in his loudest voice.

"What's the matter? Who's calling me?" rumbled the dragon, coming out of his cave.

Then the little boy said: "Tomorrow is my birthday and there will be lots of good things to eat, so please come to my party. I came all the way to invite you."

At first the dragon couldn't believe his ears and kept roaring at the boy. But the boy wasn't frightened at all and kept saying: "Please, Mr. Dragon, please come to my party."

Finally the dragon understood that the boy meant what he said and was actually asking him, a dragon, to his birthday party. Then the dragon stopped roaring and began to weep. "What a happy thing to happen to me!" the dragon sobbed. "I never had a kind invitation from anyone before."

The dragon's tears flowed and flowed until at last they became a river. Then the dragon said: "Come, climb on my back and I'll give you a ride home!"

The boy climbed bravely onto the back of the ferocious dragon and away the dragon went, swimming down the river of his own tears. But as he went, by some magic his body changed its size and shape. And suddenly —what do you know!—the little boy was sailing bravely down the river toward home as captain of a dragon-steamboat!

—by Hirosuke Hamada

The Sandal-Seller

LONG ago there was an old man and his old wife living in the country. They were very honest, but very poor. One day, near the end of the year, they heard some children singing outside. This is the song the children sang:

Oh, Mr. New Year, are you coming near?
Why, yes, I'm just beyond the mountain here.

Oh, do you bring us gifts and things so nice?
Why, yes, I've "mochi" cakes of finest rice.

It made the old man and woman feel very sad and lonely to hear the children singing about New Year's. Because this year they had no money and couldn't celebrate the New Year.

"Oh, dear," the old woman sighed. "New Year's is the day after to-morrow. And we don't have any rice at all. So we won't be able to make any *mochi* cakes. We won't even have *mochi* to eat on New Year's Day, and New Year's is not New Year's without *mochi*."

The old man too sat sadly shaking his head. But then all of a sudden he got an idea. "I know what I'll do," he said. "I made a lot of straw sandals the other day. I'll take them to town right away and sell them. Then with the money we can buy some rice and make some *mochi*."

So the old man started out for town right away, carrying the straw sandals on a long pole over his shoulder. It was a very cold day, with a strong wind and much snow. When he got to town he began to walk through the streets yelling: "Straw sandals! Straw sandals!"

But everybody was very busy and no one wanted to buy any straw sandals. He kept walking and walking, always yelling: "Straw sandals! Straw sandals!" But he never sold a single pair.

Just then another old man came along the street selling charcoal. He was yelling: "Charcoal! Charcoal!" The two old men met in the street and stopped to talk.

"How's your business?" asked the charcoal-seller.

"Terrible!" said the sandal-seller. "I haven't sold a single pair. Everybody's too busy getting ready for New Year's."

"I haven't been able to sell any charcoal either," said the other. "Come, let's walk together and see if we'll have better luck."

So they started walking together. "Straw sandals! Straw sandals!" one would yell. Then the other would yell: "Charcoal! Charcoal!"

But still they didn't sell any of the wares. It became later and later and their voices became weaker and weaker. It was also becoming much colder and snowing harder. Finally it was completely dark, and still they hadn't made a single sale, so they decided to stop and go home.

Then the charcoal-seller said: "It's really too bad to take home the same things we started out with. Why don't we trade? Then you can take home my charcoal and I can take your straw sandals."

"That's a good idea," said the sandal-seller. So they traded, and then each of them went to his home.

When the sandal-seller reached home he was very, very cold. He told the

old lady the bad news—that he hadn't been able to earn a single penny. "But at least I have this charcoal," he said, "and we can get warm."

So they made a charcoal fire and then sat around it warming themselves. But they were so sleepy that they didn't notice a tiny elf that jumped out of the charcoal and hid in their closet watching them. The elf was scarcely an inch high, but he looked exactly like the charcoal-seller the old man had met that day.

After the old man and woman had gone to bed, the elf came out of the closet and said: "I felt so sorry for this poor old man today that I gave him this magic charcoal. Every spark will turn into a piece of gold." Then the elf disappeared.

Sure enough, next morning when the old man and woman woke up, they found a great pile of gold beside the hearth. They were very surprised, but also very happy. They were able to buy plenty of rice and make very fine *mochi* for New Year's. And the old man never had to go out in the snow to sell straw sandals again.

The Robe of Feathers

ONCE there was a fisherman who lived all alone on a tiny island in Japan. He was very poor and very lonely. Early one morning he started toward his boat; there had been a bad storm the night before, but now the sun was shining brightly. As he walked along, he saw something hanging on a branch of one of the pine trees along the beach. It was beautiful and shining. He took it down from the branch and found that it was a wonderful robe made of feathers. The feathers were of all different colors, as lovely and soft

29

as the rainbow, and they shined and sparkled in the sunlight like jewels. It was the most beautiful thing the fisherman had ever seen in all his life.

"Oh, what a beautiful robe!" he said. "It's certainly a priceless treasure. There's no one else on my island so it can't belong to anyone. I'll take it home and keep it always. Then my poor home will be beautiful and I can look at the robe whenever I'm lonely." Holding the robe very carefully in his rough hands, he turned and started to carry it home.

Just then a beautiful woman came running after him. "Mr. Fisherman, Mr. Fisherman," she called, "that's my robe of feathers that you're taking away. Please give it back to me." She went on to explain that she was an angel from heaven and that the robe of feathers was actually her wings. While she was flying through the sky, the storm had come and wet her wings so that she could not fly. So she had waited on this island until the sun came out and then had hung her wings out to dry on a pine tree, where the fisherman had found them.

"So you see," she finished, "if you don't give my wings back to me I'll never be able to fly back to my home in heaven again." Then the woman began to weep.

The fisherman felt very sad for her. "Please don't cry," he said. "Of course I'll give you your robe of feathers. If I'd known it belonged to anyone, I would never have touched it." And he knelt down before her and handed her the robe.

The angel began at last to smile and her face was shining with happiness. "Oh, thank you very much, Mr. Fisherman." she said. "You're such a good man that I'm going-to dance the angel's dance for you."

Then the angel put on the robe of many-colored feathers and began to dance there before the fisherman. It was certainly the most beautiful dance the fisherman had ever seen, and probably the most beautiful dance that had ever been danced anywhere on this earth, since angels usually dance their angel's dance high up in the heavens. The air was filled with heavenly music, and the feathered robe sparkled in the sunlight until the entire island was wrapped in rainbows.

As the angel danced, she rose slowly in the air, higher and higher, until finally she disappeared far up in the blue sky. The fisherman stood watching the sky and remembering the beautiful dance he'd seen. He knew that he'd never be lonely or poor again—not with such a beautiful memory to carry always in his heart.

The Old Man with a Wen

IN A VILLAGE in Japan there once lived a hard-working old man. On his right cheek he had a big lump called a wen. One day he went to the mountain to cut wood. Suddenly it began to rain.

"Good gracious! What shall I do?" he said to himself.

Then he was lucky to find a big hollow tree where he could wait till the rain stopped. While he was waiting, his head began to nod and he fell asleep. When he woke up, he was very surprised to find it was night

34

already. In front of his tree a whole party of red and green elves were dancing.

"Aha!" cried one elf, "there's an old man in the tree." And they dragged him out of his hiding place.

"Now, old man, you must dance for us." So the old man danced his very best jig for the elves.

"Very good, very good! That was a lot of fun," said the elves, and they clapped their hands with glee.

"You must come again tomorrow night to show us your dance. Until then, we will keep your wen. Just to make sure that you do, we're going to take your wen and not give it back to you until you come and dance again." And they took the big lump right off the old man's face, thinking it must be something very precious.

The old man, of course, was overjoyed to lose his wen and left the forest singing.

When he got home, he told the story to his wife, who also was both surprised and happy. Her old husband looked so handsome without his wen.

His neighbor next door also had an ugly wen and when he heard the story, he became very excited. "I could lose my wen in the very same way!" he said, and he went to the same mountain and hid in the same tree. At last, the same elves came for their party.

"Now is the time!" said the second old man, and he jumped out of the tree and began to dance.

But he could not jig as well as the first old man. The elves were not pleased and shouted: "This dance is not as good as the one we saw last night!" Finally one of them said: "Well, we don't ever want to see him dance again. Let's give him back his wen so he won't come again."

With that, the elves took out the wen they had taken from the first old man and put it on his neighbor and chased him out of the forest. So the second old man went sadly home with two wens on his face instead of none.

The Flying Farmer

A LONG time ago there was an old farmer named Taro who lived in a village in Japan. Near Taro's house there was a wide, wet swamp where many wild ducks came to rest. Farmer Taro had made a trap out of rope, and he caught a duck almost every day.

Taro was very greedy and one night he thought to himself: "After all, only one duck a day isn't so much. How clever it would be to catch a whole lot of fine ducks at one time!"

So he made a great big trap out of a long piece of rope and fixed it so that he could catch many ducks at the same time.

Early in the morning of the next day Taro put out his new trap in the swamp. He held on to the end of the trap and hid behind a tree to wait for the ducks to come.

And then, all at once, a big flock of ducks flew down from the sky and landed right in the trap. "Tug! Twitch! Jerk! Pull! Tug! Twitch! Jerk! Pull!" Old Taro could see that he was catching many, many ducks, and he could feel them getting caught in the trap.

"Look! Look how many I have caught!" he cried, jumping up and down with glee.

About an hour later, when the sun was high in the sky, the ducks were ready to fly away. Suddenly, "Whoosh!" and they all flew up into the sky at one time.

"Oh! Oh!" Old Taro was so surprised he hung on tight to the end of his rope trap and got carried right up into the sky with the ducks.

The whole flock of ducks flew together in one group way up high, and poor farmer Taro was terribly frightened hanging onto the rope and being carried along in the air.

On and on they flew, over mountains and everything. Finally they passed over a strange village where there was a tall green pagoda with five roofs.

The old farmer waited until he got a good chance; then he let go the rope and grabbed tight onto the spire of the pagoda as he flew by it. He held on tight to the spire and cried out: "Help! Help! Help me, someone!"

Soon a great crowd of people gathered around the bottom of the pagoda. They were certainly all surprised, and began talking all at once.

"How did he ever get up there?

"Didn't you see the ducks carrying him?"

"What can we do to help him get down?"

After thinking it over, they brought a big, wide piece of cloth, and all held on to it and stretched it tight so that Taro could jump down into it. Then they all shouted up at him: "Jump down! Jump into this cloth! Jump!"

Taro looked down and was so frightened that his knees shook. But finally, he closed his eyes tight and jumped.

He was lucky and landed right in the middle of the cloth. But he was so heavy that all the round heads of the people holding the cloth were knocked together, "Bumpity, Bumpity, Bump!"

Just at that last "Bump!" Taro opened his eyes, and what do you think? He was home safe in his own bed. All this flying with ducks had been a bad dream.

But the dream seemed so real that it cured Farmer Taro of being so greedy. After that he never trapped any ducks at all and became a nice, kind gentleman.

The Magic Mortar

ONCE upon a time two brothers lived together in a little village in Japan. The elder brother worked very hard all the time, but the younger brother was very lazy and good-for-nothing. One day the elder brother went off to the mountains to work. While he was working, an old man came up to him and gave him a mortar made of stone, the kind used for grinding rice or wheat into flour.

"This is a magic mortar which will give you anything you wish for," said the old man. "Please take it home with you."

The elder brother was very happy and rushed home with the mortar.

"Please give me rice. We need rice." So saying, he ground the stick in the mortar. And all at once out came rice, bales of rice. There was so much that he gave rice to everyone in the village.

"This is wonderful! This is a great help. Thank you very much." The villagers were all very happy.

That is, everyone was happy except the lazy younger brother. "I wish I had that; I'd make better use of it," he grumbled to himself. And one day he stole the magic mortar and ran away.

"No one will be able to catch me if I can get to the ocean," he thought as he ran to the seashore.

When he reached the shore, he found a small rowboat. He took it and rowed very hard out to sea. He soon was far out and right in the middle of the big waves.

Then he stopped rowing and began to think what he wanted to ask the mortar for. "I have it! I would like a lot of nice, sweet little cakes." And he began to grind at the mortar with the stick. "Give me cake! Give me cake!" And lots of fine white cakes came rolling out of the mortar.

"My! How good they are! And what a lot of cakes I got!" And he ate every one. He had eaten so many and they were so sweet that he began to feel like he wanted to eat something salty to take the too-sweet taste out of his mouth.

So he ground at the mortar again and said: "Give me salt this time. I want salt. I want salt." And now salt came pouring out of the mortar, all white and shining. And it kept coming and coming.

"Enough," he cried, "I've had enough. Stop!" But the salt kept coming and coming, and the boat began to fill up and get heavy. And still the salt kept coming, and now the boat was so full it started to sink. And as the brother sank with the boat, he was still crying: "Enough! Enough!"

But the mortar kept on giving out salt and more salt, even down at the bottom of the ocean, and it is still doing it. And that is why the sea is salty.

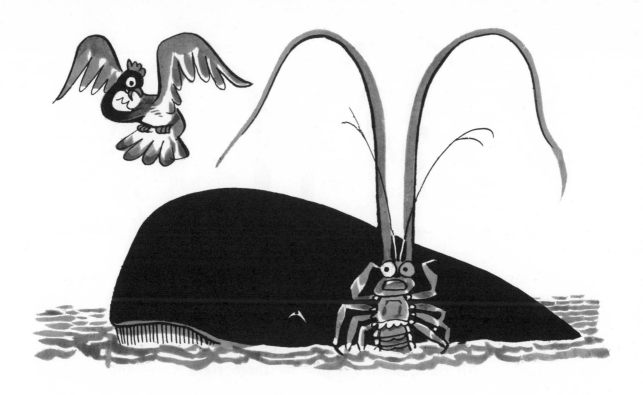

The Biggest in the World

ONCE upon a time, on an island in the ocean, there lived a big, big bird. He was big enough and strong enough to pick up a sheep, or even a cow, in one grab and fly up into the sky with it. This bird was very proud and was always boasting: "I'm the biggest in the world. If you looked all over the earth, you couldn't find another being as big and strong as I."

"Oh, no, Mr. Bird," said a sea gull one day who had just flown up from the south. "In a place in the Southern Sea there is a much larger being than you.

"What! What are you saying? Something larger than I am? You must be wrong! . . . All right, then, I'll just fly there right now, and we'll see who's biggest."

So the big bird flew off to the Southern Sea. But the Southern Sea is very wide, and no matter how far you go there seems to be no end to it. "Oh, but I'm tired!" the big bird said and started looking for a place to rest. Just in time, in the distance he saw two red columns sticking up out of the waves.

"This is just fine," the bird said, settling down with a sigh on one of the columns.

Just then the bird heard a terrible voice. "Hey!" cried the voice. "What's this? Who is sitting on the end of my feeler?" Then the column began to move, and suddenly, right from the middle of the waves, a huge lobster rose to the top of the sea, waving the feelers that the bird had thought were columns.

"Oh, what a terrible thing!" said the bird. Because he saw that the huge lobster was much, much larger than he. "I certainly lost this contest." And with that the bird flew quickly away home.

"Ho! ho! ho!" laughed the lobster. "I really frightened that bird. What fun to see the bird that thought he was so big run away like that. I'm truly the biggest in the world."

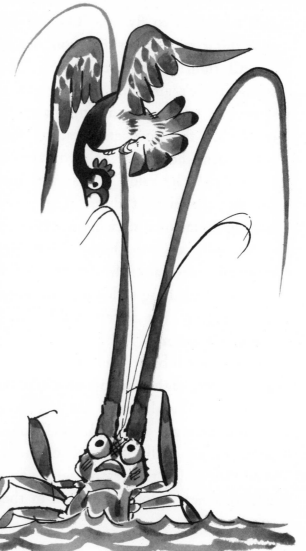

Just as the big lobster was saying this and feeling so proud, the sea gull happened to fly by. "Oh, no, Mr. Lobster," the gull said. "There is something still larger than you. You just swim farther south and you'll see."

"All right!" said the lobster, "that's just what I'll do. Such nonsense, saying there's anything bigger than I!"

So the lobster swam and swam. Finally, far to the south, right in the middle of the Southern Sea, he saw a huge mountain rising out of the water. And he could see two caves in the mountain.

"Ah ha!" he said. "Those are fine caves. They will make a good place for me, the biggest thing in the world, to sleep." And, happily wiggling his big feelers, he crawled up into one of the caves.

But what do you think! What Mr. Lobster had thought were caves in a mountain were actually the nose of a great whale!

"Oh, something's tickling my nose!" said the whale, because the lobster was wiggling his feelers inside the whale's nose. "Ka—ka—ka—choo!" the whale sneezed.

The poor lobster was blown high, high into the sky, and then he fell back down, right on top of a big rock sticking up in the ocean.

"Ouch! Ouch!" cried the big lobster. "My back is broken."

Sure enough, his back *was* broken. And that is the reason why, ever since that time, all lobsters' backs are curved as though the shell were broken. And that's also the reason why you can listen and listen but never again will you hear a lobster say: "I'm the biggest in the world."

Why the Red Elf Cried

NO ONE knows now where the mountain was, but once there was a red elf who lived on a mountain that overlooked a village. This red elf wanted to make friends with the people who lived in the village, so in front of his house he hung a sign that read: "Everybody is welcome to come to my house and eat the good candy I will give them."

One day two woodcutters passed the red elf's house and saw the sign One of them said: "Let's go in and get some candy." But the other said:

"No, no. That sign is only a trick so the elf can get us into his house and do something bad to us. Don't go inside!"

The red elf heard what the men said and called out through the window: "No, no. It's not a trick. Please come in and have some candy and be my friends." But the two woodcutters were frightened by his bright red face and ran away as fast as they could.

When the red elf saw that nobody would believe his sign he was very sad and started to take the sign down. Just then his good friend, the blue elf, came to visit him and asked why he looked so sad.

After the blue elf had heard the story, he thought for a while and then said: "I have a good plan for you. I'll go down into the village and make lots of trouble. Then you come and catch me while I am doing bad things and give me a beating. Then everyone will know you're a good elf and will want to be your friend."

So the next day the blue elf went down into the village and burst into a farmhouse. The farmer and his wife were so frightened they ran outside. Then the blue elf started breaking everything in the house. He had just broken the old woman's teapot and was just about to kick the farmer's dog when the red elf came running into the village. He grabbed the blue elf and pretended to give him a good beating. The blue elf cried with all his might.

The frightened people of the village stood at a distance and watched all this. Finally they said: "That red elf is a good elf after all. And he has lots of sweet candy at his house. So let's go and visit him often."

Why the Red Elf Cried 55

So the village people started going to the red elf's house. He was very happy to have so many new friends and he always gave them sweet candy and delicious tea. But then one day he suddenly remembered that in all this time his good friend, the blue elf, had not once been to see him. "Perhaps the blue elf is in some trouble," he said. "I'll go and see him."

Next day the red elf set out for the blue elf's house. It was far away in the mountains, but the red elf went there very quickly, riding on top of a little cloud. To his surprise, he found the blue elf's house empty and all shut up. He walked around the house several times, wondering what was the matter, and finally saw a note pinned on the front door. This is what the note said:

Why the Red Elf Cried

To my dear friend, the red elf:

I am so lonely that I am going away on a long journey. If we should keep on visiting each other the way we used to, the people in the village would know that we played a trick on them and that you didn't really beat me. So I will go far away and leave you with your new friends, the village people. Goodbye,

Your friend,
Blue Elf

The red elf read this note in silence two or three times. Then he burst into tears and cried and cried.

He had his new friends from the village and he knew he would be happy with them, but he also knew that he would always be sad when he remembered his lost friend, the blue elf, because it is good to make new friends, but it is also good to keep old friends. And this is why the red elf cried so hard.

—by Hirosuke Hamada